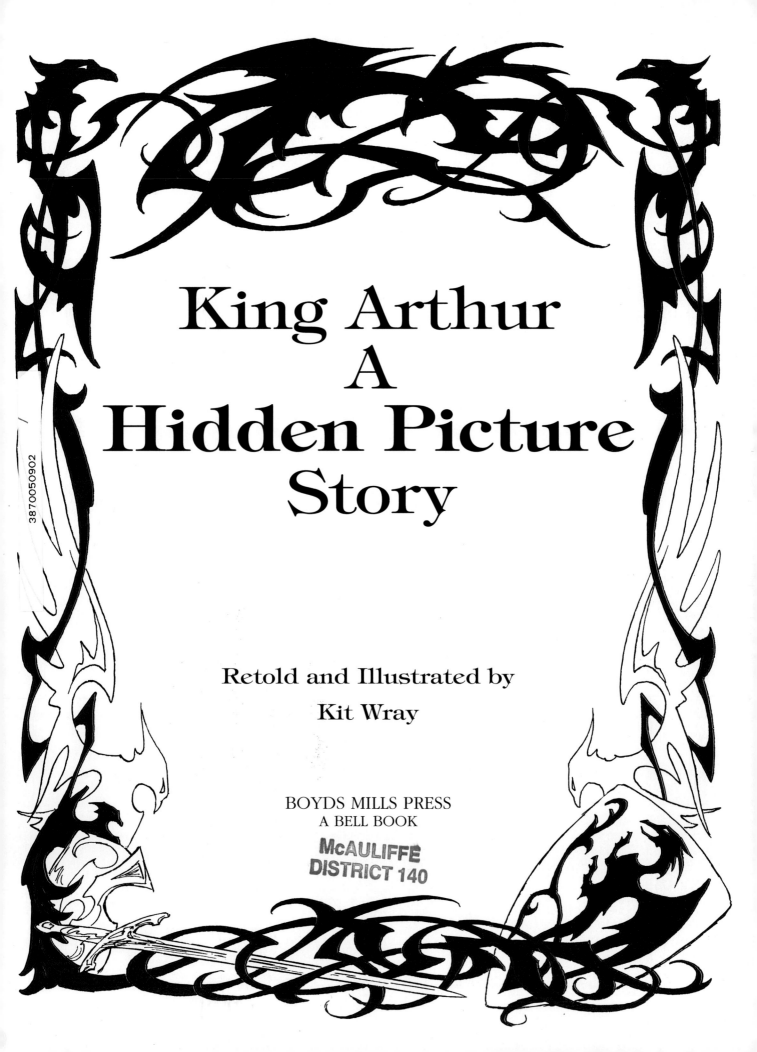

King Arthur
A
Hidden Picture
Story

Retold and Illustrated by

Kit Wray

BOYDS MILLS PRESS
A BELL BOOK

To Beth, Arlynn, and John

Published by Bell Books
Boyds Mills Press, Inc.
A Highlights Company
910 Church Street
Honesdale, Pennsylvania 18431

Publisher Cataloging-in-Publication Data
Wray, Kit.
 King Arthur : a hidden picture story / retold and illustrated by Kit Wray.
[32] p. : ill. ; cm.
Summary: The traditional legend of King Arthur accompanied by fine pen-and-ink illustrations.
Various objects are hidden within the illustrations.
ISBN 1-56397-018-X
1. King Arthur— Juvenile literature. 2. Arthurian romances — Juvenile literature. 3. Picture
puzzles — Juvenile literature [1. King Arthur. 2. Arthurian romances. 3. Picture
puzzles.] I. Title.
398.22— dc20   1992
Library of Congress Catalog Card Number: 91-76019
First edition, 1992
The text of this book is set in 14-point Century Schoolbook.
The illustrations are done in pen and ink.
Distributed by St. Martin's Press
Printed in the United States of America
10 9 8 7 6 5 4 3 2 1

When England was a very young country, a strong
king named Uther Pendragon ruled the land. After
many years, he called his people together and declared
that his infant son, Arthur, should inherit the throne.

He placed the child in the care of Merlin, his trusted
friend. Merlin was a wise man and trained Arthur in the
skills of knighthood. With Merlin as his teacher, the boy
learned the wisdom of the forests and streams and the
language of the animals who inhabited the land.

heads of a chipmunk, a pterodactyl, a falcon, and a sea lion   1

Using his magic arts, Merlin buried a magnificent sword in a stone with this inscription: "Whosoever pulls this sword from the stone is the rightful king of England."

Many strong knights wished to be king. One by one, each pulled mightily at the sword. But none could remove it.

One day, when Arthur had grown to be a young lad, he approached the miraculous stone while Merlin watched from the crowd. All were amazed as Arthur easily pulled the sword free.

Then Merlin stepped forward saying, "Behold the true king of England!" as Arthur held the shining blade aloft.

panther, heads of a doe, a dolphin, and a raccoon

Arthur was soon crowned before all the nobles and common people. Trumpets proclaimed the beginning of his reign, while the Pendragon banner floated above the cheering crowd.

Many people then came to King Arthur and complained of the wrongs they had suffered since the death of King Uther. Arthur swore to rule justly, and he soon restored lands and freedom to his people.

Though most of the people loved Arthur, certain proud barons and noblemen refused to follow the young king. So Arthur gathered his faithful knights and rode forth to secure the country under his rule.

Arthur fought valiantly at the head of his army and gained the admiration of his knights and comrades. At last his enemies surrendered, and England, under King Arthur, entered a time of peace.

squirrel, heads of a lamb, an opossum, and a pony

Arthur's sword had been broken in one of the battles. His old teacher, Merlin, found him and said, "You shall have a greater sword. I will lead you to the Lady of the Lake. Her power is both in this world and the next. We will find her in the watery realm between the worlds, which some mortals call the Land of Faerie."

At evening Arthur and Merlin came to the misty shore of a vast lake. A maiden's arm emerged from the water holding a beautifully crafted sword and scabbard. Then a radiant light came toward them over the surface of the lake. Within the brightness, Arthur perceived a fair lady, who drew near and shone before them in the moonlight.

"What do you seek?" she asked as Arthur bowed to her.

"My lady, I long to have the sword that is held there across the water."

"It will be yours for a time. But remember that its power is not of your world."

chickadee, heads of a finch, a duck, and a lamb

As the lady withdrew into the silver mist, Arthur and Merlin climbed into a small boat and pushed away from shore. When Arthur took the sword, the hand disappeared beneath the gentle waves. Upon the gleaming blade was inscribed "Excalibur." The lady's voice returned. "While you hold this sword, no enemy will defeat you. And the scabbard will save you from any mortal wound."

Arthur returned to his castle at Camelot. Each time he rode with his knights, he found that no one could stand up against the magic sword.

When Arthur visited the castle of King Leodegrance, he met the king's daughter, Princess Guinevere. Arthur was entranced with her and spoke to Merlin of marriage.

The old wizard advised against it. "Seek another to be your queen. With Guinevere, you will bring war and ruin to your kingdom." But Arthur's heart was set, and soon Guinevere arrived at Camelot for a festive reception.

sailboat, knife, shamrock, heart, hourglass

As a wedding gift, Guinevere's father sent a great round table for Arthur and his knights. They all gathered around it in the king's hall, and thus began Arthur's Fellowship of the Round Table.

Suddenly the Lady of the Lake entered the hall like a sunbeam, and a tall warrior walked with her. Everyone stared in amazement as she spoke to Arthur. "I bring you Lancelot of the Lake. He will be the greatest of knights."

Lancelot was soon to prove himself, for King Arthur had proclaimed a jousting tournament by the walls of Camelot.

Colorful banners floated in the air as each knight displayed his standard. When Arthur took his seat, trumpets heralded the jousting to begin.

With great strength and skill, Lancelot unhorsed every opponent. At last he challenged Sir Mador, who had spoken out against the new queen. Lancelot vowed to defend her honor.

feather, arrow, heads of a lioness, a goose, and a goat

From either end of the lists, the two knights leveled their lances and charged. As they drove together, Sir Mador's lance shattered while Lancelot bore him to the ground, horse and all.

Then they fell upon each other with raised swords until Sir Mador yielded and begged for the queen's pardon.

Lancelot gained Arthur's admiration that day—and also won the queen's love.

cane, caterpillar, face of an elf, rat's head   11

With his kingdom now in order, Arthur occasionally enjoyed hunting in the forest. One day he ventured out with Sir Accolon. But someone was watching.

They soon spied a white stag and followed it through the trees. By evening, they came to a river, where a ship draped in silken cloth was waiting.

All of this was created through the magic of Arthur's sister, Morgan le Fay. She feared that Arthur's growing kingdom would destroy all trace of the Faerie realm. Her plan was for Accolon to rule instead of Arthur.

dragonfly, horseshoe, frog, dove, mouse's head

The two men stepped aboard the vessel to rest for the night. Accolon was aroused to see a servant of Morgan le Fay carrying Arthur's sword and scabbard. The servant said, "Queen Morgan bids you to take these and vanquish a deadly knight who awaits you at the Perilous Castle."

Meanwhile, King Arthur awoke to find himself in a castle dungeon. A serving maid brought him a sword that looked like Excalibur. "If you would escape from here," she said, "you must overcome a powerful knight who stands now by the castle walls."

Arthur found Accolon at the castle gate, but neither man recognized the other. As their swords clashed, Arthur weakened under the savage strokes that hacked through his shield.

Then he saw the true Excalibur in Accolon's hand. With a great effort, Arthur lunged for his sword and seized the scabbard as well. His strength quickly returned, and he smote Accolon to the ground.

hand, arrowhead, fish, heads of a dragon and a wolf

Arthur then sought a hermitage where he could recover from his wounds. As he lay resting, he held the scabbard close to him to receive its healing power.

Meanwhile, Morgan le Fay felt bitter sorrow at the loss of Accolon. She went to the cloister where Arthur was sheltered and stole into his chamber.

The king was sleeping as she stood by his bed. "Alas, good brother," she thought sadly, "your power is too great. Would that Accolon had ruled."

Then she took the scabbard and rode away.

bell, moon, candle, heads of a crow and a blue jay   15

Morgan paused, then hurled Arthur's scabbard far into a deep lake. Never again would it protect him.

Arthur awoke suddenly to find the scabbard missing. Quickly, he pursued Morgan. She heard the hoofbeats coming up the path behind her.

Summoning up her magical powers, she changed herself and her horse into a huge mass of rock. Arthur passed by without noticing. He returned to Camelot, where the queen and his knights rejoiced to see him again.

chipmunk, heads of an ibis, a hawk, and a weasel

With the coming of early May, hearts were light at Camelot. Guinevere came to Arthur and asked for some knights to escort her, for she wanted to ride out and enjoy the countryside.

As the party passed near the forest, a cruel knight named Meleagant surrounded them with his warriors. They overpowered the queen's guard and took her away to their castle.

During the ambush, a young squire slipped away and returned to Camelot to report what had happened. Lancelot set out at once to find Guinevere.

cat, girl's face, heads of a dinosaur, a rabbit, and a porpoise   17

In his search Lancelot entered a wild, barren country. A path led him to the brink of a deep gorge, where a stream ran over jagged rocks far below. A tall citadel stood on the opposite cliff, and Guinevere called out to him from the tower window.

Lancelot crossed the abyss on a narrow bridge and burst through the gate with his sword drawn. Meleagant called for his men, but Lancelot struck him down and scattered the others.

fairy, axe, seal, heads of a cardinal and a goose

Then Lancelot climbed the tower to find Guinevere. Together they returned home, where King Arthur welcomed them with great joy and relief.

Arthur was unaware that he had enemies at Camelot, and he no longer had Merlin to advise him. The old magician finally had ventured deep into the enchanted world and disappeared forever.

Arthur's own nephew, Mordred, was the most dangerous of the king's foes. Mordred secretly hoped to destroy Arthur's fellowship of knights and take the throne himself.

The affection that had grown between Lancelot and Guinevere became Mordred's chance to stir up trouble. Taking several armed conspirators, Mordred followed Lancelot to the queen's tower and accused him of treason. After a grim fight on the dark stairway, Lancelot rode off.

Mordred fled to Arthur with his tale. The king's heart ached to see Merlin's prophecy coming true. But he was compelled by law to condemn Guinevere.

Early the next morning, Guinevere was led to the place of execution. Suddenly, Lancelot rode boldly into the crowd, wielding his sword against any who stood in his path. In the confusion and dim light, he struck down two of Arthur's knights. Then he pulled Guinevere onto his horse with him and spurred away to his fortress.

heads of a wood duck, a fox, and a turkey

The fellowship of the Round Table had been torn apart and Arthur was deeply troubled. But he granted pardon to the queen, and she returned to Camelot in safety.

Meanwhile, Mordred and others demanded revenge on Sir Lancelot for his actions. So Arthur left the kingdom in Mordred's charge and led his army to Lancelot's fortress in France. For months, they battled fiercely before the gates.

dog's head, numeral **7**, wishbone, sickle, ladle

Then word arrived from Camelot: Mordred had declared himself king and gathered an army to stand against Arthur. Hastily, King Arthur took ship and returned with his knights to England.

Once ashore, they marched overland until Arthur signaled his men to halt. Across a wide plain, they now faced the forces of Mordred.

Arthur and Mordred rode out in the open to confer. Both armies were instructed that if any man drew his sword, the battle would begin.

At last, the leaders agreed to call a truce. But a soldier in the ranks was bitten on the heel by an adder, and he raised his sword to kill it.

Everyone saw the signal. Before Arthur or Mordred could stop them, the trumpets sounded, and both armies raged forward with a mighty cry.

otter, heads of an elephant, a woodpecker, and a coyote

The battle lasted until evening. Under the darkening sky, Arthur stood among his fallen comrades and grieved at the loss of so many noble knights. Then he spied Mordred.

"Traitor!" cried Arthur, and he dashed forward with his spear. As the spear bore him down, Mordred swung his sword against King Arthur's helm, and both men fell.

snake, penguin, heads of a cat and an alligator

Of Arthur's knights, only Sir Bedivere remained. He carried Arthur to the shore of the lake. "Take my sword," said the king, "and cast it far over the water. I must return it now to the lady." Bedivere did as Arthur bade him, and a pale arm emerged from the water. The maiden's hand caught Excalibur and withdrew with it to the enchanted world from whence she had come.

bird, heads of a dinosaur, a sheep, and an egret

From across the lake a vessel bearing three hooded women glided out of the mist. It gently touched shore with the lapping waves. As Arthur reached out, the women received him in their arms and settled him aboard.

"Where do you take him?" asked Bedivere.

"To the Isle of Avalon," came the reply, "until his people need him again. . . ." Then a light breeze filled the sail and carried them into the setting sun. " . . . to Avalon."

Have You Found Them All?

When England was a very young country, a strong king named Uther Pendragon ruled the land. After many years, he called his people together and declared that his infant son, Arthur, should inherit the throne.

He placed the child in the care of Merlin, his trusted friend. Merlin was a wise man and trained Arthur in the skills of knighthood. With Merlin as his teacher, the boy learned the wisdom of the forests and streams and the language of the animals who inhabited the land.

1: heads of a chipmunk, a pterodactyl, a falcon, and a sea lion

Using his magic arts, Merlin buried a magnificent sword in a stone with this inscription: "Whosoever pulls this sword from the stone is the rightful king of England."

Many strong knights wished to be king. One by one, each pulled mightily at the sword. But none could remove it.

One day, when Arthur had grown to be a young lad, he approached the miraculous stone while Merlin watched from the crowd. All were amazed as Arthur easily pulled the sword free.

Then Merlin stepped forward saying, "Behold the true king of England!" as Arthur held the shining blade aloft.

2: panther, heads of a doe, a dolphin, and a raccoon

Arthur was soon crowned before all the nobles and common people. Trumpets proclaimed the beginning of his reign, while the Pendragon banner floated above the cheering crowd.

Many people then came to King Arthur and complained of the wrongs they had suffered since the death of King Uther. Arthur swore to rule justly, and he soon restored lands and freedom to his people.

3: heads of a bear cub, a lizard, and a dog

Though most of the people loved Arthur, certain proud barons and noblemen refused to follow the young king. So Arthur gathered his faithful knights and rode forth to secure the country under his rule.

Arthur fought valiantly at the head of his army and gained the admiration of his knights and comrades. At last his enemies surrendered, and England, under King Arthur, entered a time of peace.

4: squirrel, heads of a lamb, an opossum, and a pony

Arthur's sword had been broken in one of the battles. His old teacher, Merlin, found him and said, "You shall have a greater sword. I will lead you to the Lady of the Lake. Her power is both in this world and the next. We will find her in the watery realm between the worlds, which some mortals call the Land of Faerie."

5: duck, heads of a deer and a robin

At evening Arthur and Merlin came to the misty shore of a vast lake. A maiden's arm emerged from the water holding a beautifully crafted sword and scabbard. Then a radiant light came toward them over the surface of the lake. Within the brightness, Arthur perceived a fair lady, who drew near and shone before them in the moonlight.

"What do you seek?" she asked as Arthur bowed to her.

"My lady, I long to have the sword that is held there across the water."

"It will be yours for a time. But remember that its power is not of your world."

6: chickadee, heads of a finch, a duck, and a lamb

As the lady withdrew into the silver mist, Arthur and Merlin climbed into a small boat and pushed away from shore. When Arthur took the sword, the hand disappeared beneath the gentle waves. Upon the gleaming blade was inscribed "Excalibur." The lady's voice returned. "While you hold this sword, no enemy will defeat you. And the scabbard will save you from any mortal wound."

7: fish, heads of an eagle and a wolf

Arthur returned to his castle at Camelot. Each time he rode with his knights, he found that no one could stand up against the magic sword.

When Arthur visited the castle of King Leodegrance, he met the king's daughter, Princess Guinevere. Arthur was entranced with her and spoke to Merlin of marriage.

The old wizard advised against it. "Seek another to be your queen. With Guinevere, you will bring war and ruin to your kingdom." But Arthur's heart was set, and soon Guinevere arrived at Camelot for a festive reception.

8: sailboat, knife, shamrock, heart, hourglass

As a wedding gift, Guinevere's father sent a great round table for Arthur and his knights. They all gathered around it in the king's hall, and thus began Arthur's Fellowship of the Round Table.

Suddenly the Lady of the Lake entered the hall like a sunbeam, and a tall warrior walked with her. Everyone stared in amazement as she spoke to Arthur. "I bring you Lancelot of the Lake. He will be the greatest of knights."

9: mallet, pear, goblet

Lancelot was soon to prove himself, for King Arthur had proclaimed a jousting tournament by the walls of Camelot.

Colorful banners floated in the air as each knight displayed his standard. When Arthur took his seat, trumpets heralded the jousting to begin.

With great strength and skill, Lancelot unhorsed every opponent. At last he challenged Sir Mador, who had spoken out against the new queen. Lancelot vowed to defend her honor.

10: feather, arrow, heads of a lioness, a goose, and a goat

From either end of the lists, the two knights leveled their lances and charged. As they drove together, Sir Mador's lance shattered while Lancelot bore him to the ground, horse and all.

Then they fell upon each other with raised swords until Sir Mador yielded and begged for the queen's pardon.

Lancelot gained Arthur's admiration that day—and also won the queen's love.

11: cane, caterpillar, face of an elf, rat's head

With his kingdom now in order, Arthur occasionally enjoyed hunting in the forest. One day he ventured out with Sir Accolon. But someone was watching.

They soon spied a white stag and followed it through the trees. By evening, they came to a river, where a ship draped in silken cloth was waiting.

All of this was created through the magic of Arthur's sister, Morgan le Fay. She feared that Arthur's growing kingdom would destroy all trace of the Faerie realm. Her plan was for Accolon to rule instead of Arthur.

12: dragonfly, horseshoe, frog, dove, mouse's head

The two men stepped aboard the vessel to rest for the night. Accolon was aroused to see a servant of Morgan le Fay carrying Arthur's sword and scabbard. The servant said, "Queen Morgan bids you to take these and vanquish a deadly knight who awaits you at the Perilous Castle."

Meanwhile, King Arthur awoke to find himself in a castle dungeon. A serving maid brought him a sword that looked like Excalibur. "If you would escape from here," she said, "you must overcome a powerful knight who stands now by the castle walls."

13: numeral *8,* cup, goose's head

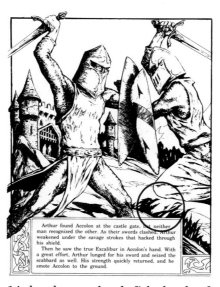

Arthur found Accolon at the castle gate, but neither man recognized the other. As their swords clashed, Arthur weakened under the savage strokes that hacked through his shield.

Then he saw the true Excalibur in Accolon's hand. With a great effort, Arthur lunged for his sword and seized the scabbard as well. His strength quickly returned, and he smote Accolon to the ground.

14: hand, arrowhead, fish, heads of a dragon and a wolf

Arthur then sought a hermitage where he could recover from his wounds. As he lay resting, he held the scabbard close to him to receive its healing power.

Meanwhile, Morgan le Fay felt bitter sorrow at the loss of Accolon. She went to the cloister where Arthur was sheltered and stole into his chamber.

The king was sleeping as she stood by his bed. "Alas, good brother," she thought sadly, "your power is too great. Would that Accolon had ruled."

Then she took the scabbard and rode away.

15: bell, moon, candle, heads of a crow and a blue jay

Morgan paused, then hurled Arthur's scabbard far into a deep lake. Never again would it protect him.

Arthur awoke suddenly to find the scabbard missing. Quickly, he pursued Morgan. She heard the hoofbeats coming up the path behind her.

Summoning up her magical powers, she changed herself and her horse into a huge mass of rock. Arthur passed by without noticing. He returned to Camelot, where the queen and his knights rejoiced to see him again.

16: chipmunk, heads of an ibis, a hawk, and a weasel

With the coming of early May, hearts were light at Camelot. Guinevere came to Arthur and asked for some knights to escort her, for she wanted to ride out and enjoy the countryside.

As the party passed near the forest, a cruel knight named Meleagant surrounded them with his warriors. They overpowered the queen's guard and took her away to their castle.

During the ambush, a young squire slipped away and returned to Camelot to report what had happened. Lancelot set out at once to find Guinevere.

17: cat, girl's face, heads of a dinosaur, a rabbit, and a porpoise

In his search Lancelot entered a wild, barren country. A path led him to the brink of a deep gorge, where a stream ran over jagged rocks far below. A tall citadel stood on the opposite cliff, and Guinevere called out to him from the tower window.

Lancelot crossed the abyss on a narrow bridge and burst through the gate with his sword drawn. Meleagant called for his men, but Lancelot struck him down and scattered the others.

18: fairy, axe, seal, heads of a cardinal and a goose

Then Lancelot climbed the tower to find Guinevere. Together they returned home, where King Arthur welcomed them with great joy and relief.

Arthur was unaware that he had enemies at Camelot, and he no longer had Merlin to advise him. The old magician finally had ventured deep into the enchanted world and disappeared forever.

Arthur's own nephew, Mordred, was the most dangerous of the king's foes. Mordred secretly hoped to destroy Arthur's fellowship of knights and take the throne himself.

19: belt buckle, heads of a pelican, a bird, a rooster, and a goat

The affection that had grown between Lancelot and Guinevere became Mordred's chance to stir up trouble. Taking several armed conspirators, Mordred followed Lancelot to the queen's tower and accused him of treason. After a grim fight on the dark stairway, Lancelot rode off. Mordred fled to Arthur with his tale. The king's heart ached to see Merlin's prophecy coming true. But he was compelled by law to condemn Guinevere.

20: shovel, dagger, book, salamander

Early the next morning, Guinevere was led to the place of execution. Suddenly, Lancelot rode boldly into the crowd, wielding his sword against any who stood in his path. In the confusion and dim light, he struck down two of Arthur's knights. Then he pulled Guinevere onto his horse with him and spurred away to his fortress.

21: heads of a wood duck, a fox, and a turkey

The fellowship of the Round Table had been torn apart and Arthur was deeply troubled. But he granted pardon to the queen, and she returned to Camelot in safety.

Meanwhile, Mordred and others demanded revenge on Sir Lancelot for his actions. So Arthur left the kingdom in Mordred's charge and led his army to Lancelot's fortress in France. For months, they battled fiercely before the gates.

22: dog's head, numeral **7**, wishbone, sickle, ladle

Then word arrived from Camelot: Mordred had declared himself king and gathered an army to stand against Arthur. Hastily, King Arthur took ship and returned with his knights to England.

Once ashore, they marched overland until Arthur signaled his men to halt. Across a wide plain, they now faced the forces of Mordred.

23: hammer, heads of a rabbit and a beaver

Arthur and Mordred rode out in the open to confer. Both armies were instructed that if any man drew his sword, the battle would begin.

At last, the leaders agreed to call a truce. But a soldier in the ranks was bitten on the heel by an adder, and he raised his sword to kill it.

Everyone saw the signal. Before Arthur or Mordred could stop them, the trumpets sounded, and both armies raged forward with a mighty cry.

24: otter, heads of an elephant, a woodpecker, and a coyote

The battle lasted until evening. Under the darkening sky, Arthur stood among his fallen comrades and grieved at the loss of so many noble knights. Then he spied Mordred.

"Traitor!" cried Arthur, and he dashed forward with his spear. As the spear bore him down, Mordred swung his sword against King Arthur's helm, and both men fell.

25: snake, penguin, heads of a cat and an alligator

Of Arthur's knights, only Sir Bedivere remained. He carried Arthur to the shore of the lake. "Take my sword," said the king, "and cast it far over the water. I must return it now to the lady." Bedivere did as Arthur bade him, and a pale arm emerged from the water. The maiden's hand caught Excalibur and withdrew with it to the enchanted world from whence she had come.

26: bird, heads of a dinosaur, a sheep, and an egret

From across the lake a vessel bearing three hooded women glided out of the mist. It gently touched shore with the lapping waves. As Arthur reached out, the women received him in their arms and settled him aboard.

"Where do you take him?" asked Bedivere.

"To the Isle of Avalon," came the reply, "until his people need him again. . . ." Then a light breeze filled the sail and carried them into the setting sun. ". . . to Avalon."

27: swan, seashell, dragon's head